All profits from sales of this book will go
towards the new community building of the
New North London Synagogue.

First published in Great Britain 2010
by Masorti Publications,
80 East End Road, London, N3 2SY

ISBN 978-0-9518002-8-7
1st Edition
Printed and bound in Great Britain

Mixed Sources
Product group from well-managed
forests, controlled sources and
recycled wood or fiber
www.fsc.org Cert no. TT-COC-002303
© 1996 Forest Stewardship Council
FSC

SHMENDRICK
AND THE CROC

Best wishes from Shmendrick

Jonathan Wittenberg

illustrated by Barbara Jackson

To childhood, chocolate and the
beauty of the Jewish year – JW

Contents

Shmendrick
Makes Challah

Shmendrick always looked
forward to Friday night.
He simply loved the taste
of challah. There was only one
problem. Did he prefer the crusty
outside with sesame seeds, or the
soft inside? He could never make up
his mind.

But this week's challah was going
to be different. Shmendrick and the
Croc had decided: it was time to
make their own.

At first things went rather well.
They mixed the flour, the yeast,

the water, a small amount of sugar and the salt. The Croc used her long nose to stir the dough until the flour began to tickle her and she sneezed. While the Croc wasn't looking, Shmendrick secretly grated a bar of chocolate and poured the brown chips into the mixture.

'Yuck! Look at all those little bits of dirt,' yelled the Croc. Shmendrick kept very quiet.

They left the dough in the warm airing cupboard to rise. It seemed to take forever and ever. They were dying to look, but knew they had to be patient.

After an hour they opened the

cupboard door. The dough had definitely risen! In fact, it had climbed right out of the bowl. Long snakes of pale challah pastry with chocolate flecks were crawling across the sheets, towels and all the other cleanly folded laundry.

'We're going to get into trouble for this!' said the Croc. But, to their surprise, it was quite easy to scoop up all the dough. Only a tiny trace of flour was left behind.

They rushed downstairs to make their challahs.

They rolled out long thin sausages of dough. That was great fun and very easy.

But the next stage proved more difficult. Neither Shmendrick

nor the Croc knew how to plait their lengths of dough together. Shmendrick got in a terrible muddle and accidentally rolled a spoon and a miniature packet of raisins into the middle of his challah.

It was then that the thought occurred to him: 'What makes a challah a challah?' he asked the Croc. 'I mean,' he tried to explain, 'how is it different from any other kind of bread?'

This was a question for which they needed the rabbi. So they rang him up at once, getting challah mixture all over the telephone.

'I beg your pardon,' said the rabbi, 'but I can't quite hear what you're saying'.

'Sorry,' said Shmendrick as he removed a large lump of dough from the phone. 'What we want to know is, what makes a challah a challah?'

'Well,' replied the rabbi after listening carefully, 'I think what you've done is very special. But there are still three things you have to think about.'

'Yes?' said Shmendrick and the Croc eagerly.

'First of all, have you made your challah in an extra special way,

because you love Shabbat?'

'Yes!' they both said, and
Shmendrick added, 'I even grated
chocolate into the dough!'

'Excellent,' said the rabbi. 'Next,
have you broken a little piece off
your dough and said the blessing
to God who commanded us to give
away a portion from our baking?'

'No,' they answered. 'Why should
we do that?'

'To remind us of what it says in
the Torah,' said the rabbi. 'In the
Land of Israel, whenever people
baked bread they used to give some
to the priests. We can't do that any
more today. So we take a little piece

of dough about as big as a mouse's nose and put it in the bottom of the oven to burn, as a reminder of what used to be done.'

Shmendrick was relieved. He'd thought for a moment that they would have to give away half their baking. But then he remembered: 'What was the third thing?' he asked anxiously.

'That's most important,' said the rabbi. 'When we make something really special for ourselves we should always make a little extra for others. Bake one of your challahs for someone else and give it to a mouse or a crocodile who's

14

sad or who isn't feeling very well.'

'Is that what makes the challah Jewish?' asked Shmendrick.

But the rabbi simply said, 'Shabbat Shalom,' and left them to finish their baking.

Shmendrick, the Croc and the Lights

It was the close of Shabbat, so Shmendrick and the Croc had special permission to stay up late.

It had been a wonderful day. They'd played and prayed, listened to stories, and eaten as much as their tummies could hold.

They'd just finished their third Shabbat meal with a large cup of cocoa and a chocolate biscuit. Two treats at once were unheard of on an ordinary weekday. But Shabbat was special. (Shmendrick even

secretly dipped his chocolate biscuit
into his cocoa and licked the melted
end.)

Night was falling and the stars
were shining in the sky. It was time
for Havdalah.

'I'm going to hold the candle,' said
Shmendrick.

'I'll be the first to smell the
spices,' responded the Croc. She
didn't argue about holding the
candle because she hated it when
the hot wax dripped onto her nose.

After the prayers, the singing,
and the blessings over the drink,
the spices and the light, they
had a special custom. Instead of

wine, they used
whisky. When they dipped the
candle in it to put it out, it set the
alcohol on fire. The flames danced
in the darkness in wonderful
shades of orange and blue. 'Shavua

Tov,' they sang as they watched the flames rock and skip around the plate until at length they jumped up towards the sky and disappeared.

'Next Friday night the flames will come back down and light the Shabbat candles,' said the Croc. 'Shabbat begins with flames and ends with flames; it starts with the Friday night candles and ends with the Havdalah candle.'

Shmendrick, however, was puzzled. 'But the light on the Friday night candles is so different from the flame of the Havdalah candle.'

The matter troubled him. He determined that next Shabbat he would sit and stare straight into the flames and work out what was special about each of them.

Friday night soon came. The candles were lit, the blessing said, and Shmendrick and the Croc settled down to watch. The flames were still and tranquil: 'Shabbat Shalom,' they seemed to say. 'We are Shabbat peace.' Shmendrick and the Croc could feel the stillness within their hearts, as if inside them was a little mirror in which the candles were reflected.

Several walks, games, prayers

and large meals later (including
generous slices of chocolate cake)
came Havdalah. The tall candle
with its many wicks hissed, then
began to burn. Flames of many
shades sprung up and danced; there
were red flames and orange flames,
blue flames and scarlet flames, a
leaping mixture of glowing colours.
'We are the flames of the working
week,' they seemed to say. 'We melt
metals and turn the wheels of great
machines. We make and we create.'

'I understand why the Friday
night candles are the beginning of
Shabbat,' said the Croc. 'They make
me feel so peaceful.'

'I understand why the Havdalah
candle is the beginning of the
working week,' said Shmendrick. 'It
makes me want to bounce and jump
and try to do everything at once.'

But then he remembered that
he'd promised to tidy up his room
as soon as Shabbat was over. 'I do
love the Friday night candles best,
though,' he added, as he turned for
a last piece of chocolate cake.

Shmendrick's Rosh Hashanah Card

As far as Shmendrick was concerned there were two problems with most of the letters which came in the post. They looked very boring in their dull printed envelopes and they were almost always for other people.

But one day there was a letter waiting for him. 'Shmendrick,' it said on the address label, and the pink and yellow envelope looked interesting. So he took it up to his room and opened it in secret.

It read:

Dear Shmendrick,

As you know, it will soon be Rosh Hashanah.

This year we are making a special card to send to all our friends. We want to write in it five New Year wishes from five very special personalities.

That's why we've contacted you. Would you please write back to us as soon as possible with your own personal New Year's wish for the birthday of the world?

We will be happy to send you ten free cards as well as your very own mystery gift.

Yours sincerely,
The Mazal Tov Card Company

Shmendrick was very excited. He felt proud that he'd been asked to write a greeting for this unusual card. But what was he going to say?

He began to think.

'Dear God, this year can I have lots of chocolate?' didn't sound quite right. Maybe it would be better if he put, 'Dear God, this year can you give lots of

chocolate to everyone in the whole wide world?' But he wasn't really sure about that either.

'Maybe I should write something about peace,' he thought. But that sounded like what everyone else always did.

'Maybe I should wish everyone happiness.' But that sounded boring.

After a whole hour of thinking, he still couldn't make up his mind. So he decided to phone the rabbi.

'What should I put in that card?' he asked in desperation.

'I'm afraid I can't tell you,' replied the rabbi.

'Why not?' asked Shmendrick, feeling most disappointed.

'Because,' explained the rabbi, 'whoever it was who sent you that letter wanted to know what *you* would write, not what *your rabbi* would tell you to write. The only advice I can give you,' he continued, 'is that you have to say something which you really feel'.

Shmendrick went back to his room. He was a little upset with his friend the rabbi. Surely he could have given him a bit more help! Maybe he wouldn't go to synagogue this Rosh Hashanah after all.

But then he began to think

further. The rabbi had said,
'Something you really feel'. What
did he feel? What did he actually
wish for the world?

Flowers – well yes, they were
very pretty.

Friends – yes, they were really
important.

Chocolate – he did like it very
much. But in his heart of hearts
he knew that it wasn't the most
important thing in the whole
universe.

Then he had it. He rushed to find
a pencil and he wrote:

*I want the whole world to be the
kind of place where we can all sit*

*with friends in peace and happiness
and enjoy a very large bar of
chocolate followed by a thick slice of
chocolate cake.*

Before he had time to change
his mind he put his reply in the
envelope provided, posted it that
very day and settled down to wait
for his '*very own mystery gift*'.

Shmendrick and the Sound of the Shofar

Rosh Hashanah was only a week away and Shmendrick went to look at the shofar. There it was, lying on its side on the shelf. Ever since he was very little, he had loved its sound. It was one of those long, curved shofars and Shmendrick thought it looked sad, curled up all alone.

'Shofar, shofar, tell me what you're thinking,' said Shmendrick.

At first the shofar was silent, as if it was keeping a secret.

'Shofar, shofar,' he said again,

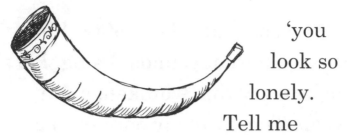

'you
look so
lonely.
Tell me
what you're
thinking.'
'I'm preparing
my sounds for Rosh
Hashanah and I'm
dreaming of all the
stories I'm going to
put in them,' said the shofar
quietly, as if it didn't really want to
talk.

Now Shmendrick's interest was
truly aroused. 'What stories?' he
asked, eagerly.

'You see,' said the shofar, 'I have three different sounds. I sing, I make a cry that's broken, and I weep. Those are my only sounds and the only time people listen to them is on Rosh Hashanah. If people only listen to you once each year you have to be careful what you say.'

Shmendrick could hardly imagine it. He liked to talk all the time.

'Is it a secret, or will you tell me your stories?' asked Shmendrick. 'Tell me the story of the sound that's broken.'

'Well,' said the shofar sadly, 'There are the sticks on the grass

and the bricks on the ground.'

'That's not a story!'

'Oh, but it is! Actually it's two
stories. The sticks on the grass are
what the little bird saw when it
came back to its nest and found it
broken and its chicks all gone. The
big birds or the cheeky squirrels
must have done it. The mother bird
squawked and cried.

'And the bricks,' the shofar
continued sadly, 'are what the
small girl saw when she ran back
home and found that something
terrible and strong had broken
down her house. There were dust
and clothes and toys, all mixed up.'

'I think that should be your crying sound,' said Shmendrick, suddenly feeling little and upset.

'It is that too,' the shofar continued, 'because where things are broken there are almost always tears. But this year my weeping note is going to be about the young puppy.'

'The young puppy?'

'Yes, the puppy who was looking everywhere for the child he loved. But that child's family didn't want the puppy any more and left him

all alone on a strange street corner far

from home.
Do you know,
there are lots
of people in
the world as
lost and sad
as that little
puppy?'

'It must be
hard to be a
shofar and think about all those
things,' said Shmendrick.

'That's why I have that big hollow
space inside me. I keep lots of
stories in my middle. But once a
year on Rosh Hashanah I tell them
and hope that people will listen.

'But you, you look so sad now,'
said the shofar to Shmendrick.
'Shall I tell you one of the stories
about my long singing note? I think
it'll cheer you up.

'There are going to be ducks in
my singing note, swimming under
willow branches in a river, and a
swan with tiny cygnets under its
wings. And there's going to be a
little boy eating the biscuits his
grandmother made and laughing
at the tales she tells him. And I'm
going to have someone who plays
music...'

Shmendrick was going to listen
very carefully indeed on Rosh

Hashanah. He wanted to hear
every single story in the shofar's
notes, though he wondered if
anyone ever did.

Shmendrick looked up.
But the shofar had fallen
silent, dreaming
of its stories.

Shmendrick's Yom Kippur Letter

It was late at night and everyone else was long since in bed. Shmendrick sat alone in the kitchen, deep in thought. His friend the rabbi had told him that before we ask God to forgive us on Yom Kippur we have to make peace between ourselves.

Shmendrick thought hard.

He knew he was supposed to ask his family and friends to forgive him, but he couldn't think of anything really bad he'd done.

He also knew he had to forgive

everyone else for what they had done to him. Here, several examples came to mind. There was the time his chocolate had mysteriously disappeared from his drawer. There was the occasion when his sweet box was suddenly empty. There were several other little mysteries too.

So he took a piece of paper and wrote hastily in large writing:

dearEveryone,
I forgive you All.
love,
Shmendrick

He folded the letter and placed it in an envelope which he labelled 'Everyone' in large blue letters.

He went to bed feeling very pleased with himself.

Then in the night he had a dream.

He was at the Croc's birthday party. She had a huge cake, covered in rich chocolate icing. It was kept safely out of sight until the grand moment when the candles would be lit. But for Shmendrick the temptation was simply too great. While everybody else was playing 'pass the parcel' he crept into the larder and cut himself a slice.

It was so delicious that during musical chairs he secretly took another, larger piece.

When the cake was brought out there was a terrible fuss. 'Who stole those giant slices?' everyone asked. 'Not me,' said Shmendrick. 'It must have been the rabbit.'

In his dream Shmendrick saw the rabbit sitting in tears while everyone called her a thief. Shmendrick awoke with a

shock. His conscience felt dreadful. It was all perfectly true. He *had* eaten those slices of cake and he could even remember how delicious they'd tasted. He had blamed the rabbit. And he'd never owned up to anybody.

Suddenly he remembered his letter. It was the middle of the night and everyone was still asleep. He went quietly back downstairs to the kitchen and opened the envelope.

He thought for a moment, then tore up the paper and began again on a new sheet, in much smaller writing:

Dear Everyone,

It was me who ate that cake. Rabbit, please forgive me.

I'm very sorry for all the naughty things I've ever done.

Sorry.

Love,

Shmendrick

PS I forgive whoever it was who took my sweets and chocolates.

He put the letter in the envelope and climbed slowly up the stairs, desperately hoping that he would have no more bad dreams.

Shmendrick and the Most Important Thing in the World

Shmendrick and the Croc had been told that Yom Kippur was the most important day in the year. But that left them with a question: what was the most important thing in the world which they should be thinking about on that most important day?

'I know what you're going to say. You're going to say *chocolate*', said the Croc. But she was only teasing, even Shmendrick could tell that.

Still, how were they to know what

was the most important thing in all
the world?

'We'll ask the rabbi,' said
Shmendrick.

But the Croc thought that wasn't
a good idea. They should begin by
trying to find out for themselves.
'We'll go and explore. We'll look
very carefully and listen very hard.
Maybe we'll be able to discover for
ourselves what matters more than
anything else.'

Out in the street everyone
seemed to be walking very fast.
A man rushed out of a shop, then
ran back inside and came out even
faster with a large bag: 'Where

46

would I be if I'd forgotten that!' he shouted over his shoulder to the shopkeeper. A lady almost flew across the pavement into the bank. A dog tugged at its lead. Everybody seemed to be behaving as if what they were doing was far more important than anything else and as if the world would fall to pieces without it.

Shmendrick and the Croc turned off the road into the quiet of the woodland. After a while they came to a large tree whose branches swayed and sighed in the wind.

'Why do you sound as if you were crying?' asked the Croc.

47

'That's because my leaves have
lovely colours and I don't want to
lose them too quickly,' replied the
tree. 'You see, people come here to
look at me when they're tired and
miserable and the shades of my
leaves make them happy. Because
of that the colours make me happy
too.'

This did seem rather important to
Shmendrick and the Croc.

Just in front of the tree they saw
a squirrel digging hurriedly in the
earth.

'Why are you digging so busily?'
asked Shmendrick.

'I'm digging,' replied the squirrel,

catching
his breath,
'because if I don't
bury my acorns now, there won't be
enough to eat in the winter; not for
my children, nor for their friends,
nor for me, nor for anyone else who
needs to eat. I hate to see anyone
going hungry and there are hungry
creatures everywhere. So I'm doing
what I can to stop it.'

That, too, impressed Shmendrick and the Croc.

On a seat nearby they saw an old man who looked as though he was dreaming. 'What are you dreaming about?' they asked him.

The man turned to look at Shmendrick and the Croc and a warm smile illumined his face. 'Young animals,' he said, 'that's a very special question, so I'll give you my most special answer. You see, I come here every day I can and I give myself half an hour to dream. I dream about my family and friends and about all the people I love, especially the children. And

as I dream about them, I thank
them and pray for them to be well
and I send them my love in my
thoughts. And I dream, too, about
the children who have no one to
dream about them.'

The old man smiled again and
fell silent. His words seemed to
Shmendrick and the Croc to be very
important indeed.

It was late by the time
Shmendrick and the Croc got home.
Their feet were tired but their
hearts were full. Their thoughts
were so busy with all the important
words they'd heard and sights
they'd seen, that they'd long ago

forgotten the question about what
was the most important thing in all
the world.

Shmendrick and the Croc Sleep in Their Succah

Shmendrick and the Croc were ever so excited. That night they were going to sleep in their own Succah for the very first time!

They had made the Succah all by themselves. They had fixed the poles to form the corners, built the walls from planks of wood and laid bamboos across the top on which to put the leaves and branches for the roof.

Then they had gone round the

garden together. 'Will you please let me have some branches for my Succah?' Shmendrick asked the tall bay tree, because bay has a lovely scent.

'May I use your leaves to cover my Succah?' the Croc asked the laurel bush next to the path.

They had asked the rose for some of its red hips, the pear tree for a twig with three grey green pears still hanging on it, and the late chrysanthemums for permission to use them to decorate their Succah. A good Succah, they knew, had not only to be strong but also beautiful.

Beautiful it was! That was why

they brought down their sleeping bags and lay down, each in their own corner, staring through the branches at the stars.

But it wasn't at all the way they had imagined it would be. First they began to feel cold and damp, then frightened and bad tempered. 'I'll never, ever sleep in a Succah again,' thought Shmendrick in his misery.

That was when the rustling noises began. A small creature with a long tail came bouncing over the roof and started to chew the best and most beautiful pear.

'Who are you?' Shmendrick

wanted to say, but he was too scared.

Next there was a scratching sound through the leaves on the floor. Tiny, damp feet crawled straight past the Croc's nose, but neither of them could make out who the animal was. Then a fox glided in on silent paws. Even the wind stopped; not a leaf in the whole Succah stirred.

The fox looked at Shmendrick and the Croc: 'Don't be frightened,' she said. 'I'm almost always awake at night and I love to go wandering, but I've never seen anywhere like this. What kind of place is it and

can I play here too please?'

'I also like it here,' said the squirrel from its perch on the pear.

'Me too,' piped up the mole from the floor and several mice from in between the leaves. 'We've never seen anywhere like this either. Can we too play here please?'

Shmendrick and the Croc let out their breath. 'It's a Succah,' they explained. Soon they were playing with all the other animals. When the birds began to sing at dawn, their happiness was complete.

'What's this? What's this?' sang the robin, hopping in through the leaves. The finches came in threes

and fours. The thrush sang, 'Tell us, tell us, what a Succah is!'

At that moment Shmendrick forgot all the explanations they had taught him in cheder. But in his heart he knew the answer. 'It's a house made out of everything God has given us,' he said. 'We built it from the branches and the leaves.'

'And it's a house of sharing,' added the Croc, feeling for a moment that there was no creature in all the world who couldn't become her friend.

Shmendrick Dances
With the Torah

Shmendrick was lying on his bed late at night, but he couldn't get to sleep. He tried lying on this side and he tried lying on that side, but nothing would help.

It wasn't because his tummy was too full. In fact, he thought he'd been rather good about what he'd eaten, especially since it was Simchat Torah. He'd only had three biscuits and one bar of chocolate.

But that was the point: it was Simchat Torah, and he just didn't

understand. How can you dance
with the Torah? How can anyone
dance with the Torah?

Shmendrick wasn't very good
at dancing anyway. He got out of
time with the music or tripped over
someone else's feet, which made
him unpopular. But that wasn't
the point. Shmendrick couldn't
understand how *anyone* could
possibly dance with the Torah. You
can dance with your friends. You
can dance with your family. You
can dance in a circle, or even on
your own. But how do you dance
with the Torah? Torahs can't dance!

Just then Shmendrick heard a

little voice calling out to him in the dark. 'Shmendrick!' it said, 'Shmendrick!'

He sat up, feeling frightened. It definitely wasn't the Croc's voice. He listened sharply for any further sounds.

'Shmendrick! Shmendrick!' There it was again.

'Don't be afraid, Shmendrick,' said the voice in a gentler tone. 'I'm your friend. Have you forgotten me?'

'Who are you then?' he asked, fear turning into surprise.

'It's only me! Open the cupboard in the hall and come and look!'

Shmendrick felt comforted by the sound of the voice. He got out of bed and walked towards the hall. It was then that he remembered the old Torah which the family kept in the little cupboard which served them as an ark.

Shmendrick opened the door and looked at the Torah.

'It's Simchat Torah, Shmendrick, and I want you to dance with me!' said the Torah.

Shmendrick was silent for a moment. Then he said, 'But, little Torah, I don't know how to dance with you. That's why I couldn't sleep!'

'I know,'
said the Torah,
'and that's why I wanted to
talk to you. Will you let me teach
you how to dance with me?'

Shmendrick looked at the Torah
and nodded.

'Right then. This is how I would like you to dance with me. When you see something kind to do, like feeding the birds, or looking after someone who's ill, or making someone lonely feel at home, I want you to do it. That's how you take a step towards me in the dance.

'When there's something you know you shouldn't do, like lying, or saying nasty things, or taking someone else's chocolates, I want you not to do it. That's how you take a step backwards in the dance. That's how you dance with me, Shmendrick. Do you think you can learn how to do it?'

Shmendrick was listening very carefully. He'd never heard of a dance like this one before.

'Will you dance with me, Shmendrick?' the Torah asked again. 'Will you dance with me, not just on Simchat Torah, but all your life?'

'I'll try,' said Shmendrick very quietly.

Chanukkah Presents

Shmendrick and the Croc were discussing the all important subject of Chanukkah presents.

'No, no, Shmendrick,' said the Croc, 'not the presents you want to get, but the presents you're going to give to other people!'

'I think I'll give everybody a small bottle of oil,' said Shmendrick. 'It'll remind them of that miracle about the oil which burnt for eight days and they can use it to make latkes and doughnuts and things.'

But the Croc wasn't impressed.
'Oil!' she said. 'What kind of a
present is that? Who wants oil?
How about some special coloured
candles for the chanukkiah?'

This sounded like a very
attractive idea. But there was
something else they had to decide
on first.

'Who are we going to give
presents to?' wondered Shmendrick.

There were aunts and uncles,
cousins and friends. So off they
went to the shops with a very long
list.

It was while they were shopping
that Shmendrick remembered

something really important. He
was thinking about his uncle
when it all came back to him. This
uncle lived on his own and last
year Shmendrick had gone round
to see him on the third night of
Chanukkah so that they could
light the candles together. They
had placed the Chanukkiah in the
window just as they were supposed
to do, then lit the candles with all
the right blessings and songs.

It was only after they'd been
sitting watching for several
minutes that Shmendrick noticed
the reflections. He could see not
one but two chanukkiahs, and not

three but six candles, as well as
two shammashim. But when he
looked more carefully, especially
if he squinted a little, he could see
four, even five sets of candles, each
one seemingly further away in the
darkness, all of them shining out
as if they were signalling to each
other.

'Yes,' said his uncle, 'I often look at those reflections. You can think of them like generations, little Shmendrick.'

'Generations, uncle?' asked Shmendrick in surprise.

'Yes, Shmendrick, generations. I look at the reflections and I think of my great-grandparents smiling at my grandparents, who smile at me. They lived and died long ago, but the same Chanukkah lights which burn for us used to burn for them too. The lights link us together.'

All this came swiftly back to Shmendrick as he stood there in the shop. He turned to the Croc and

said, 'I want to buy mirrors to give as my Chanukkah presents!'

'Mirrors!' she exclaimed. 'What on earth do you want them for?'

Shmendrick did his best to explain. Mirrors, he hoped, were cheap. All one had to do was to put a mirror behind the Chanukkiah and there would be lots and lots of reflections, lots of souls and spirits waving in the flames of the reflected candles. A mirror would make a wonderful present. Whoever he gave it to would think it was just like magic.

The Croc looked thoughtful. 'I don't think it'll work like that,' she

said. 'There are some things you can't make happen,' she added, wisely. 'People only appreciate them if they happen by themselves.'

Shmendrick paused for a moment, his mind filled with the memory of all those Chanukkah candles shining in his uncle's window. The Croc was right.

'What I'd really like,' he said, 'is for all of us together to light the candles by the window so that we can sit quietly and watch them and think of our great-grandparents waving to us in the flames'.

It was the Croc's turn to look thoughtful. 'You'll have to show

me,' she said. 'I've never seen anything like that before.'

'I certainly shall,' said Shmendrick. Then he added, in a fresh spurt of enthusiasm, 'If we don't need mirrors, then I'm going to buy chocolates for everyone instead, including for myself.'

Shmendrick and His Friends Talk About Doughnuts

Shmendrick loved doughnuts. In fact, his favourite game was to suck out the jam without getting the sugar stuck on his nose. But there was a question which had been worrying him ever since he was very little. Everyone knows that doughnuts have jam inside. But how did that jam get there?

Shmendrick had two new friends: a duck and a hedgehog. So he asked them both as they were sitting

together enjoying the light from
the Chanukkah candles: 'How does
the jam get into the middle of a
doughnut?'

'That's easy,' said the hedgehog.
'When anything happens to me, I
just roll up into a ball. So I expect
a doughnut does the same. They
put the jam in front of it, then the
doughnut sits down on top and
curls up over it. It makes itself into
a round ball with the jam right in
its middle.'

'You don't know anything,' said
the duck. 'Doughnuts can't curl up.
They're only made of dough. That's
what *dough nut* means! I'm a duck

and when I want to eat something
I peck a small hole in it with my
beak. I expect that the bakers who
make the doughnuts ask for ducks
like me to come and help them. The
ducks peck holes in the dough, then
the baker fills the doughnuts with
jam and puts them in the oven.

'I'd like to help the bakers next
year,' added the
duck with a little
quack, as an
afterthought.

'I don't believe either of you,' said Shmendrick.

'So what's your great idea then?' asked the duck and the hedgehog together.

'It's all very simple,' said Shmendrick. 'You see, I've got quite a big tummy. When I want to put something inside it, I eat it. So I expect that doughnuts do the same. They swallow the jam and it finishes up right in their middles. That's how doughnuts get jam inside them.'

'Nonsense,' said the duck. 'Doughnuts can't swallow.'

Meanwhile, the argument

had made them all hungry. So,
forgetting for a moment how the
jam had got there, they sat down
in front of the candles and had two
more doughnuts each.

The Last Night of Chanukkah

It was the last night of Chanukkah. The eight candles of the final day were burning down.

Shmendrick and the Croc were sitting watching the flames. They had enjoyed Chanukkah. They'd given presents and sent money for tzedakah, just as one should.

But now the festival was almost over.

There was a little hiss, and a ring of smoke climbed up towards the ceiling from the Croc's Chanukkiah.

The last piece of wick from one of
Shmendrick's candles glowed red
and orange.

Shmendrick was sad. The number
of lights reflected in the window
was getting smaller; the flames
were flickering and disappearing.

Now only two candles were left
burning.

'What happens when things end?'
he asked.

The Croc was thinking the very
same thought: 'Where does the light
go to when the candles have burnt
out?'

Neither of them knew the answer.
They both liked Chanukkah and
they didn't want it to be over.

'Look!' said Shmendrick. The
last candle on his Chanukkiah had
burnt right down. The flame was
licking the wax out of the bottom
of the holder and dancing brightly.
It was bigger than it had ever been

before. Then suddenly it leapt up into the air and vanished.

'Maybe the flames go to heaven,' said the Croc.

'I don't think so,' said Shmendrick. 'When I finish a bar of chocolate that means that it's all gone. It's not in heaven; it's in my tummy!'

'Chocolate and flames are different,' observed the Croc.

'But the Chanukkah lights could still be somewhere inside us,' said Shmendrick thoughtfully. 'Not in our tummies, of course, but somewhere else inside.'

'If so, they'd burn us, just like the

wax burnt my nose the night before last,' said the Croc who hadn't forgotten how much it had hurt.

But Shmendrick was no longer listening. He was remembering what had happened when his grandmother had died. 'She'll live on inside us,' his mother had said.

Shmendrick was wondering if lights could live on inside one too.

The last candle went out. All that was left was a tiny spark of orange in the black end of the wick.

'I've loved these lights,' said the Croc. 'They've made me feel warm and happy and bright. They've made me feel quiet and at peace.'

'Maybe those thoughts,' said Shmendrick quietly, 'are the lights which live on inside us'.

Shmendrick and the Croc Celebrate Tu Bishevat

The next day was going to be Tu Bishevat, the New Year for Trees.

'What does a tree like for its birthday?' Shmendrick wondered.

'How about if I make a cake in the shape of a leaf or a branch,' suggested the Croc.

'Trees don't eat cakes!' said Shmendrick.

'Except for mud cakes,' replied the Croc quickly. But both of them agreed that making a birthday cake

probably wasn't the best plan.

'I know,' said Shmendrick, 'let's go outside and have a look at the trees in the garden. Maybe they'll give us an idea'.

'I don't think it's really fair to ask them,' said the Croc. 'Then their presents won't be a surprise.'

'That's true,' agreed Shmendrick, 'But maybe just by looking at them we'll think of what to do.'

They went outside into the muddy garden and stopped next to the first tree they saw. Its bark was cold and drops of water ran down the trunk. But the buds on the branches were bright, full of

energy for the coming of the spring. A blackbird hopped across the earth beneath it, looking for the last remains of fallen fruit.

Shmendrick and the Croc stared at the tree. Suddenly they turned towards each other; they'd had the very same idea at exactly the same moment.

'This poor tree must be lonely. There isn't a single other tree in the whole of this big garden!'

'I know,' said Shmendrick, 'let's go to the park and dig up a tree. Then we can bring it back here and plant it and our tree will have a friend.'

'That's called stealing,' observed the Croc.

'OK then, we'll buy a tree,' said Shmendrick.

But they'd never bought a tree before. They didn't even know in what kind of shop to look, and anyway, trees were too large for mice and their friends to carry.

'Trees grow from seeds,' said the Croc. 'Let's plant some seeds instead.'

This was a sensible suggestion. But what kind of seeds turned into trees? They decided to conduct a thorough investigation. They would search the entire house and garden,

then meet again next to the tree in half an hour, bringing everything they'd found.

The Croc brought a walnut. 'I think walnuts grow on trees,' she suggested. 'This one looks really good, so maybe we can plant it.'

Shmendrick had an apple. 'I think the pips might grow,' he said sensibly.

He also had a banana. 'I like them better than apples,' he said, 'But I don't think bananas can grow into trees.'

The Croc had found an acorn on the pavement. 'I love oak trees,' she said.

Shmendrick had brought a box
of chocolates filled with nuts. 'If
nuts can grow, maybe these ones

will turn into chocolate trees,' he suggested hopefully. But even he realised that nature didn't work like that.

Meanwhile the wind came up and the tree swayed slowly to and fro above them, as if it was nodding in agreement and saying to itself, 'What a wonderful idea that Shmendrick and the Croc are planning to plant seeds.'

But it was going to be a very long time indeed before the tree had a friend.

Shmendrick, the Croc and the New Moon of Adar

It was Rosh Chodesh, the New Moon of Adar. Shmendrick and the Croc loved new moons and couldn't wait to see the tiny, bright crescent in the sky.

But that wasn't why they were so eager this particular time. What really excited them was the song they had learnt at school: 'When Adar begins there's lots and lots of happiness,' and today was the start of the month of Adar.

'Happiness is sweets and

chocolates,' said Shmendrick, thinking of Purim when he was allowed to eat as many as he wanted.

'My teacher says that happiness is peace and quiet,' said the Croc. Then she added, 'But I think happiness is music, dancing and beautiful things'.

'The rabbi says happiness is doing what's good and right,' said Shmendrick. 'I don't think the rabbi really knows what chocolate is.'

Shmendrick had several coins in his pocket and he couldn't wait to spend them. 'Let's go for a walk and buy some chocolates,' he suggested.

So off they went. The sun was out
and the day was bright. The earth
was just that little bit warmer
than before and the birds were
singing more loudly. In the park,
yellow crocuses stood like groups
of sentinels in the grass. The buds
were getting fatter on the trees.
Shmendrick and the Croc couldn't
help feeling happy.

'You're right about beautiful
things,' said Shmendrick to
the Croc. 'And I'm right about
chocolate,' he added as he opened
the door of the sweet shop.

It didn't take them long to spend
their money. Ten minutes later

they were back on the park bench with their chocolate bars.

They were eating happily when a dog came running up. When he saw that they were eating he sat down to watch. He stared at the chocolate in their hands. He stared at their fingers as they broke off small pieces. He stared as they lifted them to their

mouths. Then he stared at them as they chewed.

'That dog's making me feel guilty,' said the Croc.

'Me too,' said Shmendrick. 'He's stopping me from enjoying my treat. But I bought it with my very own money and it's mine.'

The dog took no notice. He simply sat there and stared.

'Let's give him some chocolate, then we'll all feel happy again,' said the Croc. So they gave the dog a generous piece. He ran off with his prize and gulped it down. But half a minute later he was back, staring at them all over again.

'Happiness,' said Shmendrick, as he picked up the very last piece of chocolate, 'is giving to others, but having just enough left over for yourself'.

'That bit was mine!' cried the Croc in horror. But even as she said the words, Shmendrick dropped it on the ground. Quick as a flash, the dog picked it up and ran off, his tail wagging happily.

Shmendrick felt very guilty; he didn't know what to say to the Croc. But just then he remembered what the rabbi had said. 'Happiness,' he reminded her, 'is doing what's right and fair!'

Shmendrick and the Croc Make Their Own Megillah

Shmendrick and the Croc were very excited. In three days' time it would be Purim.

'We'd better get out our Megillah,' said Shmendrick.

They searched the whole house but, try as they might, they simply couldn't find it. They were very upset and disappointed.

But then the Croc had a great idea. 'Let's create our own!' she exclaimed.

'Make our own Megillah!'

muttered Shmendrick, unimpressed. It sounded like a great deal of work and not a lot of fun. 'You mean, write down every single word?' he asked.

'Of course not,' said the Croc. 'That would be far too hard. I mean design our own. Just imagine, we could do a three-dimensional Megillah with puppets and real food and everything! That really would be great!'

'That's a brilliant idea!' said Shmendrick, catching her excitement at last.

But first they had to solve a practical problem. On what should

they place their Megillah? They
put together the kitchen table,
the dining room table and the
table from their room, which they
dragged all the way down the
stairs by themselves. That meant
that they had three tables all in a
row on which to put their three-
dimensional Megillah.

Shmendrick started to read from
a short book he found, called 'What
Happens in the Megillah':

*King Achashverosh made a party
for 180 days. Then Vashti the Queen
made a party, too.*

So they piled food high for the
feasts and put little puppets

all around it, with chocolates and carrots and crisps in their mouths, and a sign saying 'Party in Shushan Town'. That filled the first half of the first table.

'I bet they ate different kinds of things back then,' said the Croc.

'It doesn't matter,' answered Shmendrick, who was already looking forward to when the Megillah would be over and he could help himself to the food.

The King gathered all the girls to choose a new queen, read the Croc. So they put out dresses and crowns and lipstick, with a special chair for the winner, above which they wrote

'Esther's Throne' in large letters.

'What do you think happened to Vashti, the old queen?' asked Shmendrick, wondering if they should make a little cottage in the country just for her.

For Haman they put people lying flat on their faces wherever he went. They used a box for a desk, with a feather for his quill pen and paper for that nasty letter he wrote about the Jews whom he hated. 'What about a computer for him to email everybody?' asked the Croc.

But Shmendrick was thinking about Mordechai. 'I think I'll use a Torah with a kippah on for him.'

By now they had filled the whole of the second table as well. They were happy and excited.

Esther invited the King and Haman to a party, read Shmendrick.

'More food!' groaned the Croc.

'No,' said Shmendrick, 'only drinks this time'. And he borrowed the two best bottles of whisky in the house. 'People won't mind,' he said, 'because we're doing it for something holy'.

That night the King couldn't sleep, they read.

'I think he had toothache,' said Shmendrick.

'No,' said the Croc, 'I expect he was scared. When I can't sleep it's usually because I'm scared.'

'But kings don't get frightened.'

'They do,' answered the Croc, 'when they think someone's going to chop off their head. I expect Achashverosh thought Haman was going to do exactly that to him.'

But Haman was punished and told to lead the King's horse through the streets with Mordechai seated on it.

They used their toy horse, and to prove that it really had been all around the town they took little pieces of dried guinea-pig pooh and

scattered it along the path which
the procession had followed.

Then they piled up chocolates for
the party Mordechai gave when he
became the King's chief adviser and
all the Jews were saved.

*They sent gifts to the needy and
presents to their friends*, read

Shmendrick. 'I'm going to put a tin at the end of the table to collect coins for the poor.'

There before them was the whole story of the Megillah modelled in thrones and puppets and food.

'Now that we've made our Megillah,' said Shmendrick, 'we can look forward to going to all those parties and eating everything up!'

Shmendrick
and the Horse

Shmendrick was worried.
'Croc!' he called out from
his bed, 'Croc!'

'What's the matter, Shmendrick?
It's the middle of the night,'
moaned the crocodile crossly.

'I just can't get that poor horse
out of my mind. I keep dreaming
about it; I wonder what happened
to it in the end.'

'Which horse?'

'The horse in the Megillah, of
course.'

But the Croc couldn't remember

and Shmendrick had to remind
her. He told her about how King
Achashverosh asked Haman what
should be done to a person the King
wanted to reward. Haman replied
that the person should be dressed
in the royal robes, crowned with the
King's crown, seated on the royal
horse and paraded round the town.
The only problem was that the
man King Achashverosh wanted to
honour was not Haman himself, but
Mordechai, whom Haman detested.

'So Haman had to lead Mordechai
round the town on the royal horse
and I bet he treated that poor
animal really terribly just because

he hated Mordechai so much.
That's what those humans do:
when they're angry with someone
they take it out on their animals. I
can't sleep because I keep thinking
about it. I wonder if horses can cry.'
Shmendrick gave a big sigh.

It was then that the Croc had an
idea.

'You know on Purim,' she said,
'you have to give gifts to the poor
and send food to your friends.
Well, do you think we could give
something to horses to tell them
that we care?'

Shmendrick really liked the idea.
He loved preparing those little gifts

called Mishloach Manot. But he wasn't sure if it was allowed to give them to horses.

That's why at eight o'clock the next morning the phone rang in the rabbi's study.

'You want to send Mishloach Manot to a horse?' The rabbi had heard of many strange and wonderful doings in his time, but this was something new.

'Well,' he continued after giving the matter some thought, 'I really can't see why not. But I think it has to be done as an extra gift. You see,' he explained, 'on Purim you have to give money to the poor and send

gifts of foods to friends. I think you can definitely send some to a horse, but it has to be an extra portion.'

Shmendrick and the Croc were not at all disappointed. 'That means we can buy even more hamantaschen and chocolates and sweets to make presents!' they cried.

'And,' added the Croc more quietly, 'we'll also need some hay'.

The next day, which was Purim, Shmendrick and the Croc were seen swinging little baskets of all kinds of food as they walked along, visiting the hospital, their friends and, last but not least, a field with a horse and two tiny Shetland ponies.

Shmendrick's Matzah

Shmendrick didn't want to buy matzah for Pesach. He wanted to make it himself.

'I'm sure it didn't come in those square boxes when the Children of Israel were in Egypt,' he said to the Croc. 'They had to make it themselves. So we should make it ourselves as well, otherwise we won't be able to say that it's the same bread as our mothers and father ate when they were slaves in Egypt!'

The Croc couldn't fault

Shmendrick's argument. But she had a strange suspicion that he had something else in mind as well. It was when she overheard him talking on the phone to the rabbi that she realised she was right.

'Why not?' he was asking.

'Because,' answered the rabbi, 'matzah is called the bread of poverty'.

'So I can't put any chocolate into my dough at all, not even the tiniest, littlest grated pieces?' said Shmendrick in a tone of obvious disappointment.

'I'm afraid not,' said the rabbi. 'You see, our ancestors didn't have

any chocolate when they were slaves in Egypt.'

Shmendrick couldn't imagine life without chocolate. Then a further worrying thought went through his mind. 'What about jam, or sugar? Is there anything sweet at all I'm allowed

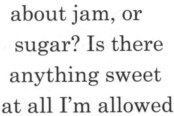

to put into my matzah for the Seder?'

'No,' said the rabbi, 'they didn't have anything like that in Egypt. Life was very hard for slaves back then and it's still the same for those poor people who are slaves today.'

Shmendrick thought for a moment. 'If I saw a slave I would certainly offer him some of my chocolate. Do you think there were any kind Egyptians who gave the Children of Israel nice things to eat?'

This wasn't the kind of question the rabbi was usually asked. 'There are always decent people,'

he replied slowly, 'and some of
them must have given the slaves
food when they saw how miserable
they were. Not everyone is hard
hearted.'

'So can I put a little chocolate in
my matzah dough after all? Just
in memory of those good people?'
asked Shmendrick, his voice rising
in expectation.

'No, I'm afraid you definitely
can't. You see, our teachers tell
us that matzah must be made as
simply as possible. That's why it's
baked out of flour and water only,
mixed very quickly and put into a
burning hot oven so that it won't

rise. It's hard and has very little taste.'

'I think I'll do without matzah this year then,' said Shmendrick sadly.

'I'm sorry, Shmendrick, but you're not allowed to do that either. The Torah tells us that we have to eat matzah at the Seder. But,' said the rabbi suddenly as a new thought entered his mind, 'what are your three favourite foods?'

'Chocolate, chocolate cake and chocolate pudding,' replied Shmendrick instantly.

'Well, how about putting a little of each of them (kosher for Pesach

of course) in a bowl right next to your matzah at the Seder?'

'Yes, yes, yes!' said Shmendrick quickly, licking his lips.

'Wait a minute, I haven't finished yet,' the rabbi went on. 'Then, when you're eating the matzah you can look at them and think: "My ancestors didn't have these lovely foods when they were slaves in Egypt, so I won't eat any of them either."'

Shmendrick thought that this was a terrible idea. Even at the other end of the telephone the rabbi could sense his disappointment. The Croc smiled to herself as she

121

secretly listened in.

'But,' concluded the rabbi, 'afterwards, when we remember how our fathers and mothers left Egypt and became free, then you could maybe allow yourself a little piece of chocolate and a morsel of cake and a small spoon of chocolate pudding – to put yourself in mind of what freedom tastes like too!'

Shmendrick Makes His Own Maror and Charoset

Every year Shmendrick and the Croc liked to prepare something special for the Seder. But this year they just couldn't think of what to do.

All at once the Croc had an idea. 'Let's make our own charoset and put something delicious into it for everything sweet in the world.'

Shmendrick thought this was a brilliant plan.

'And I suppose we should make our own maror too,' continued the

Croc. 'We could take a bowl and put into it something bitter for every horrible thing we can think of.'

Shmendrick felt that wasn't quite such a great idea.

Nevertheless, they took one bowl for everything sweet and another for everything bitter and sat down to decide what to put in them.

First of all, they thought about the charoset.

They looked out of the window and saw the trees in blossom. 'I'm putting in an apple for all the beautiful things which grow in the spring,' said the Croc.

'I'm adding honey for all the

124

foods which taste sweet,' said
Shmendrick. Even he understood
that no one makes charoset with
chocolate.

'Are there any kinds of food which
sing,' wondered the Croc, 'because
music is certainly something
sweet?'

'Maybe we should add some wine,'
suggested Shmendrick, 'And I'm
going to
put in a
raisin

for each of my friends.' But on second thoughts he decided to pour in the whole packet because maybe one day everybody would become friends.

'I like lovely smells,' said the Croc, breathing in the spring air by the window. 'I'm putting in spices for all the wonderful scents and perfumes in the world.'

'I like home,' said Shmendrick. 'What can I add for that?'

'I like freedom to do what I want,' said the Croc. 'What can I put in for that?'

The bowl for charoset was speedily filled and the mixture

126

was sticky, but delicious.

But Shmendrick and the Croc grew quiet as they began to think about the maror. They looked at one another and agreed: they should have done the maror first. They didn't feel like thinking about bitter things now.

'Maybe we should just leave it,' suggested Shmendrick. But that didn't feel quite right.

'I don't like it when people cry,' he said.

'I don't like it when something really hurts,' said the Croc.

'Or when I cut myself.'

'Or when people have accidents.'

'Or when you see all those pictures of children who have nothing to eat.'

'Or when animals are treated cruelly.'

'I hate it when things just aren't fair.'

'I don't like it when people fight.'

'And I hate it when everyone shouts.'

They had soon thought of plenty of things which were bitter and sad. But they still didn't know what to put into the bowl.

'I think we should choose just one horrible taste for them all,' suggested the Croc.

In the end they chose a very sharp raw onion. It made them cry and its juice stung their tongues as soon as it touched them.

'I'm not going to have any of it at the Seder,' said Shmendrick with a shudder. Inside, though, he knew that this was wrong.

'Perhaps on second thoughts,' he corrected himself, 'I'll have just a little and I'll taste it for just one moment, because otherwise it wouldn't be fair.'

'What wouldn't be fair?' asked the Croc.

'It wouldn't be fair,' said Shmendrick, speaking mainly to

himself, 'if we ate so many nice things and enjoyed all those lovely flavours while lots of sad and horrible events were happening to others'.

The Croc agreed: 'We need to think about all those sad things too.'

That was why on Seder night they took the maror and kept it in their mouths for just a moment, then swallowed it down amidst their tears. After that they helped themselves to spoonful after spoonful of charoset made of apples and raisins and honey and cinnamon and sweet wine.

Shmendrick, the Croc and the Four Mice at the Seder

Shmendrick and the Croc invited their new friends, four young mice, to the Seder.

The first mouse was ever so interested. Her eyes missed nothing at all. 'Look at that matzah!' she said. 'It's all full of holes. Does that

mean that other mice have nibbled it already? Is that because on this night we all have to share?'

'That's a good question,' said Shmendrick, 'but the holes weren't made by nibbling. Matzah is bread which isn't allowed to rise. We put rows of holes in it to keep it flat and low.'

'Why do we do that?' asked the first little mouse.

'Because,' said the Croc, 'that's what they fed us when we were slaves in Egypt long ago. And hard, dry crumbs are all many poor mice still get in the world today. So we eat matzah tonight and think about

how life must feel like for them.'

The second mouse was feeling cross and didn't want to be at the Seder at all. 'It's boring and my tail hurts and I want to go to my nest,' he complained to himself. But out loud he just said, 'Let me go home, please let me go home!'

'That,' said Shmendrick, 'is exactly what the slaves said in Egypt, when they asked God to let them go free.'

'Free!' said the second little mouse. 'Who cares about freedom? Just let me go to bed!'

'But isn't that what freedom means,' replied Shmendrick, 'having your dinner and going to your own nest and curling up safely in your bed? That's what God did for us when we were slaves in Egypt long ago. God made us free and took us home to the Promised Land.'

The third mouse was frightened and shy. So she hopped into the middle of a bowl of green stalks and rolled up as small as she could.

'Maybe nobody will notice me here,' she thought. But just then somebody picked up the very same leaves she was sitting on and dipped them – and her – in a great big puddle of grey water. 'Ugh!' she screamed, 'that tastes all salty!' And she began to cry.

But the Croc turned to her and told her in a very kind voice, 'Don't be afraid, because that's salt water

and it's supposed to remind us of
tears. Slaves have to work hard all
day long; they don't get much food
and they haven't a corner to call
their own. We're supposed to cry
when we think about them.'

*The fourth
mouse*
simply
couldn't
sit still.
'These
prayers and
songs are taking
a very, very, very long time,' he
said to himself. So he waited until

no one was looking, then quickly climbed up a bottle of wine. But as he was about to sit on the top he slipped and slid down and dropped right into a bowl of sticky fruit.

'This is rather nice,' he said to himself as he licked himself clean. 'I wonder what it is!'

'That,' said Shmendrick, 'is called charoset and it's like the mud we used in Egypt to fix the bricks together when we were slaves to Pharaoh'.

'Nice, that mud,' said the fourth little mouse still licking at the lumps stuck to his fur.

'Yes,' said Shmendrick, 'because

it's made of sweet fruits to remind
us how kind we were to one another
when we were working so hard in
the land of Egypt'.

So Shmendrick, the Croc and
their four new friends all had large
helpings of charoset.

Afterwards, their faces sticky but
their hearts happy, they settled
back down to sing the songs of the
Seder.

Shmendrick's Seder Night Dream

Shmendrick was enjoying the Seder. But he was only a little mouse and the evening seemed to him very, very long. It got so late that he fell fast asleep at the table.

Maybe it was because he had eaten a whole piece of matzah, which was hard and dry and tasted of nothing. Or maybe it was because he had secretly drunk four entire glasses of wine, although everyone had told him not to, and that he was much too young, and

that it wasn't allowed. Or perhaps
it was because he had had a third
and then a fourth and finally a
fifth helping of that sweet, sticky
charoset which was almost, but not
quite, as delicious as his favourite
chocolate. Or perhaps it was
because it was simply so very, very
late.

But fall asleep he did.

It was then that he had his
dream. It was a very bad dream
indeed, the worst that he had ever
dreamt.

Someone was shouting at him:
'Faster, faster. I said "Run!" I don't
call that running!'

In his dream Shmendrick tried to run, but his feet felt heavy and they kept sinking into the thick sand. In front of him was an enormous pile of bricks. He knew that he was meant

to carry them across to the place where other slaves were building a wall so high that he couldn't see anything beyond it.

But the bricks were heavy and his back and shoulders ached.

'I said move! Now move, and make it quick!'

The slave-driver had a big wooden stick in his hand which frightened Shmendrick. Once again he tried to run and once again his feet sank into the sand. He looked around him. All he could see was the wide open desert, the mound of bricks, the giant wall and hundreds of other slaves just like himself.

He called out to one of them, 'Help me, help me please!'

'Who told you that you were allowed to talk?' cried the slave-

driver. 'Open your mouth one more time and I'll hit you with this stick. Work! That's all the likes of you are good for, work!'

Shmendrick was so frightened that he dropped the bricks he was carrying. They fell on his foot and hurt him and the shock of the pain woke him up.

'Help me, help me, help!' cried Shmendrick loudly as he opened his eyes.

'What's the matter, little Shmendrick?' This time the voice was gentle and kind. Shmendrick realised that he was back again among his friends at the Seder table. Everyone was staring at him.

'You shouted out,' said the same gentle voice. 'You must have fallen asleep at the table and had a bad dream.'

Shmendrick looked around him at all the smiling, concerned faces.

'I think I must have dreamt that I was a slave in Egypt. It was terrible. My whole body hurt, I couldn't do the work, my feet kept slipping in the sand and a huge, nasty man was screaming at me.'

'But you're free now and you're here and safe with us,' said friendly voices from all around the table.

'I'm so happy that I'm free,' said

Shmendrick. 'It must be terrible to be a slave.'

'That's why we have the Seder,' said his friends, 'to thank God that we're free.'

'Yes,' said Shmendrick, helping himself to a piece of chocolate to calm himself down. 'I don't ever, ever want to be a slave for the whole of the rest of my life.'

He was so happy to find that his dream hadn't been real. But he hadn't forgotten it either.

Shmendrick, the Croc and the Lag Be'Omer Bonfire

'Bring something to burn, something to barbecue and something to shine brightly in the light of the fire,' said the rabbi when he invited Shmendrick and the Croc to his Lag Be'Omer bonfire.

'Lag Be'Omer,' they asked, 'What's that?'

'It's the 33rd day of the counting of the Omer, which is the time between Pesach and Shavuot,' came the reply, 'and it's a special

and exciting day!' The rabbi didn't offer any explanation about why one should have a bonfire. Maybe he didn't know. Or maybe it was a secret he didn't want to share.

'Something to burn,' wondered Shmendrick. 'Maybe I could take my school homework.' But in his heart he knew this wasn't a good idea.

'I think we should take something which will smell nice in the fire,' suggested the Croc. So they chose a branch of dried bay leaves and some twigs of thyme.

'Something to barbecue': that was a much more interesting question.

'Marshmallows!' said the Croc.
'But I'll have to put them on a very,
very long stick or else my nose will
get burnt!'

It wasn't such a simple decision
for Shmendrick. Even he realised
that you can't barbecue chocolate.
'How about if I have the lump
of chocolate on a spike and you,
Croc, hold some biscuits in a net
underneath it so that when the
chocolate melts it drips down and
makes chocolate biscuits.' They
couldn't quite work out how to do it
so that the net wouldn't catch fire,
but it had to be worth a try.

The last item was by far the most

difficult. 'Why do you think the rabbi wants us to bring something to shine in the fire?' asked the Croc.

'I don't know,' replied Shmendrick, 'it's probably some sort of religious thing'. But it sounded rather fun.

The two of them simply couldn't agree on what to choose. In the end they made their own decisions and kept them secret from one another.

The bonfire was wonderful. The bay leaves blazed and for several minutes the whole fire smelled of spices. The marshmallows, which they held safely on very long sticks, were quickly toasted and eaten.

149

Shmendrick's
chocolate dripped everywhere,
but some of it did land on the
biscuits and the net did not get
burnt.

'So what have you brought to
shine in the light of the flames?'
asked the rabbi.

The Croc showed him her tiny
necklace with the Hebrew letters
of the word *chai*, life, hanging on
it. The silver shone and sparkled
as they stood at a small distance
from the edge of the fire. All of a
sudden the flames sank low and the
jewellery couldn't be seen any more.
But then the fire flared up again
and the Croc's *chai* shone out,
spelling 'life'. It was a wonderful
moment.

'And what about you?' the rabbi
asked Shmendrick. The little
mouse had thought and thought.
In the end he had brought one of
his favourite toys, a small model

globe that one could spin round
and round. He held it up near the
flames.

As the fire burnt up or faded low,
different countries shone out in the
dark. Shmendrick turned the globe
around. Everyone watched: 'There's
Australia!'; 'That's America!' they
shouted. Somewhere was the very
place where they were standing,
only far too small to see.

'I thought it would be nice,' said
Shmendrick, 'if we could light up
the whole world'.

'With life,' added the Croc,
holding up her *chai*.

The rabbi smiled.

Shmendrick and the Croc Pass a Sleepless Night

Shmendrick and the Croc were extremely excited. Never before in their whole lives had they ever stayed up all night. But this was Shavuot, the festival of the giving of the Torah, and Shavuot was different. On this night, they had been told, it was a special mitzvah to stay up until dawn and study Torah.

They had no intention of going to bed at all.

First, they ate lots of cheesecake.

Shmendrick liked his in thick slices with cream on top. The Croc preferred the sort with raisins inside.

'Is cheesecake one of the Ten Commandments then?' she asked.

'Only if you break them by stealing it,' answered Shmendrick with his mouth full. He wasn't sure if it had been a good idea to eat so much. It had made him tired. But he pulled himself together. This was the night when he wasn't going to sleep at all! His eyes weren't going to shut for even one single moment until dawn.

'What are we going to do

now?' asked the Croc, suddenly wondering if this sleepless night was going to be all that interesting.

'We're going to watch the Torah of course,' replied Shmendrick with conviction. He went to their special Ark and gently carried down the small Sefer Torah they had been given. 'Here, we'll open it and put it on the table.' He unrolled the scroll and they sat down to look at the letters.

A thin moon shone in the sky; everything was quiet outside. Shmendrick and the Croc realised that keeping awake wasn't going to be easy.

'What do you think is the most important thing in the whole Torah?' asked the Croc.

'Maybe it's that bit about thanking God for food,' said Shmendrick instinctively. 'After all, if our tummies weren't full we couldn't stay alive.'

'You would say that,' said the Croc. 'Trust you! I think it's that bit about all our heart and all our soul.' She yawned quietly.

By now Shmendrick's head was on the table. He was already dreaming.

In his dream the Torah was growing bigger and bigger. It rolled

itself all the way to its beginning and the very first letter, which was the letter *bet*, climbed out of the scroll and took him by the hand. 'I'm the first letter of the story of creation,' it explained in a kind and gentle voice, 'and I'm going to show you night and day, earth and sky, land and sea, and all the plants, the animals and the birds'. The letter *bet* then led Shmendrick on a wonderful walk through forests, along rivers and down to sandy coasts.

No sooner had they come back home than the Torah scroll rolled itself on until the letter *aleph*

climbed out. 'I'm the first letter of *I am the Lord your God*', it explained. 'I speak to everybody in the whole wide world. I rather like talking to you. Remember that, because all your life I'll be trying to speak to you.' Shmendrick thought that sounded rather strange. But before he could even reply, the letter *aleph* clambered back into the Torah and the scroll rolled itself shut.

It felt to Shmendrick as if a very long time had gone by. He raised his head and looked up. He was back in his own room. The night was gone and a fine, pale light was brightening the windows. The birds

were singing eagerly in the garden.

'You went to sleep before I did,' cried the Croc. 'I saw you with your head on the table!'

'Me! Asleep!' Shmendrick was indignant. 'Just you ask the Torah. The Torah and I have been talking to each other all night!'

Shmendrick's Dilemma

'It's not fair, it's just not fair.' Shmendrick was angry and upset.

Here he was, in the first week of his holidays, ready to enjoy himself after a year of far too much hard work. First of all he wanted to eat chocolate. Then he wanted to go swimming. After that he couldn't yet decide, but he wanted to have lots and lots of fun.

And then he heard about Tisha Be'Av. 'You mean,' he said in disbelief, 'that we're meant to be

sad and to fast and not eat or even drink anything at all for a whole, entire day, right in the middle of our holidays?'

The rabbi told him that he was too young to fast. 'But perhaps,' he suggested knowingly, 'you could avoid snacks between meals and special treats like chocolate.'

'Why should I?' asked Shmendrick crossly.

The rabbi explained why Tisha Be'Av was a sorrowful day. It was because of all the bad things that had been done to the Jewish people and all the tragedies that had happened in the world.

'But it's my life and I don't want to be sad!' cried Shmendrick.

The rabbi said nothing. He simply looked gently at Shmendrick, as if to say, 'is that really true?'

Shmendrick went out for a walk to think things over and calm himself down. But he'd no sooner entered the lane that led to the park when he heard a cry. 'Miauw!' it said in a pitiful voice, 'Miauw!' Shmendrick saw a tiny kitten lying all on its own under a bush. It looked very, very hungry. It had obviously been there for a long time.

Shmendrick rushed home to fetch

a bowl of milk. The little kitten
drank voraciously. He wondered
what to do next. After all, the
kitten would soon be hungry again.
Also, any passing dog might bite it.

Just then he heard a voice from
behind him say, 'Poor little thing!
I'll take it home and look after it,'
and a lady with a kind face scooped
the animal up and held it carefully
in her arms.

Shmendrick came home in a very
different mood: 'I wish I was as
kind as that,' he thought.

Scarcely three minutes had gone
by when the Croc came in crying
and sat down next to him. The

tears rolled slowly down her nose
and fell softly to the floor. She
didn't say a single word.

It took Shmendrick a long time to
find out what the matter was. The
Croc had also had an adventure.

She'd been sitting in the garden,
thinking. After a while she heard a
rustling noise and saw a blackbird
hopping up and down among the
leaves under the hedge.

'Hello,' she said to the bird, but
the bird ignored her. It didn't fly
away; it kept on

hopping this way and that. After a while the Croc saw that one of its wings looked all wrong. The feathers hung down at a strange angle. She realised that the wing was broken and the bird wasn't able to fly.

'It didn't even say "Help!" It just looked hopelessly at me. It must have been terrified.' The Croc began to cry again.

Shmendrick's heart ached. He felt that it was both feeling sad and growing bigger at the same time. It struck him suddenly that perhaps a sorrowful day like Tisha Be'Av was important after all.

'What shall we do for that poor bird?' he asked the Croc.

Shmendrick and the Croc Plan a Holiday

'We're going away!' said Shmendrick to the Croc.

'We're going away!' said the Croc to Shmendrick with great delight.

But Shmendrick wasn't really delighted. Somewhere, somehow, he didn't feel quite right about this holiday.

'I'm going to swim! I'm going to get all muddy!' cried the Croc. But Shmendrick was listening to a different voice, a voice that came from deep inside.

That voice was
saying, 'Why should you
be having a holiday when so many
people are having such a miserable
time in the world? Why should
you have an extra treat when so
many crocodiles and Shmendricks
and people are sad, or hungry and
alone? It's just not right!'

'I'm going to swim! I'm going to get all muddy!' cried the Croc again. But she could sense that Shmendrick wasn't really listening any more. 'What's the matter with you?' she asked in a troubled tone.

'I don't know,' said Shmendrick. 'I feel bad about this holiday thing. I don't think we should go.'

'Spoilsport!' said the Croc. 'What's wrong with having a good time and enjoying ourselves? I've been looking forward to this holiday so much and now you're saying that we can't go! Why not?'

The Croc's comment made Shmendrick feel even worse. So

he decided to do what he often did when he didn't know what to do: he phoned the rabbi.

'Shmendrick,' said the rabbi, 'what's troubling you now?' And he listened to what the young mouse had to say.

'Well,' he answered thoughtfully, 'the truth is that both of you are right. The Croc is perfectly correct. There is nothing whatsoever wrong with enjoying life. Life is special and important and it doesn't go on forever. A very famous rabbi called Hillel once said, "If not now, then when?" I think he meant, "Do good and enjoy life while you can!"

'But,' continued the rabbi, 'that brings me to the other point. Shmendrick, you're right too. It's very selfish to have a good time and forget everyone else. That's why we need to share a part of everything we enjoy with others. This is especially important when we're giving ourselves a treat. It's especially, especially important when other people – or mice – are having a particularly hard time.'

The rabbi paused. There was a moment's quiet on the line. Then he continued: 'So, Shmendrick, have you worked out what you should do?'

But Shmendrick still wasn't sure, and out of the corner of his eye he could see the Croc watching him unhappily.

The rabbi listened to the silence: 'I believe you can work it out for yourself now, Shmendrick. You don't need me to tell you, do you?'

And at that very moment Shmendrick knew exactly what to do!

Acknowledgements

This project is the brainchild of Susan Reuben and Sarah Manson who encouraged me to turn my love of telling Shmendrick stories into a book. They selected the tales, helped me improve the writing and did all the important work.

There was only one real choice of illustrator: Barbara Jackson. I knew that she'd have the skill and understanding to capture the cheeky charm of Shmendrick, the Croc and their friends. I'm so grateful for her delightful drawings.

Andrea Fraga and Sophie Pelham worked hard on the design and cover of the book. My children, Mossy, Libbi and Kadya, and the pupils of Gan Alon pre-school, were the first to hear these stories and were often very frank about their quality.

But it all began with a parcel sent to me by my friend Frau Gudrun Hoerner. Shmendrick jumped out of it and has remained with me ever since. I would like to acknowledge the manufacturers, Förster Stofftiere, who cannot possibly have known that their product would one day become the chocolate-loving hero of a collection of Jewish stories.

Rabbi Jonathan Wittenberg

173

RABBI JONATHAN WITTENBERG was born in Glasgow and grew up in London in a family of Jewish refugees from Germany who loved stories, especially his grandfather Georg, a rabbi, and his mother Lore. Stories have always been part of the Jewish tradition and telling stories about the festivals of the year was a natural part of his work, and pleasure, when he became a rabbi.

Shmendrick bounced out of a brown paper parcel one day and immediately became a friend. When Jonathan married Nicky, their bridesmaids carried Shmendrick and the Croc in their baskets of flowers. When the children were born it was only natural that the little yellow mouse should become the chief story-teller at the Sabbath table.

The themes and values treated with humour in these tales – kindness, honesty, the joy of the festivals – parallel the subjects explored, with more rigour but similar warmth, in Jonathan Wittenberg's writing for adults. He is rabbi of the New North London Synagogue and Senior Rabbi of the Assembly of Masorti Synagogues. A busy teacher, speaker and writer, with a strong involvement in inter-faith relations, he above all enjoys community and contact with people of all ages. He and Nicky have three children and very numerous animals.

Jonathan Wittenberg's writings (for adults) include:
The Three Pillars of Judaism: A Search for Faith and Values;
SCM Press Ltd, 1996
The Eternal Journey: Meditations on the Jewish Year;
Aviv Press, 2004
The Silence of Dark Water: an Inner Journey;
Robin Clark Limited and Joseph's Bookstore, 2008

BARBARA JACKSON is a graduate of St Martin's School of Art and works in the disciplines of painting and printmaking. She has been awarded five prizes in Printmaking and held two successful one-man exhibitions. She has exhibited three times at the Royal Academy Summer Exhibition.

A member of the Southbank Printmakers Cooperative in London, she also has work in galleries around the country, including Hampstead, Eastbourne, Surrey and Birmingham.

Barbara is currently teaching Foundation Studies at The Institute in North London, and runs an art workshop at the Holocaust Survivors Centre. She is married with two children and four grandchildren. Her husband says she also makes a mean fruit cake.